DONUTS AND DISASTER

A SANDY BAY COZY MYSTERY

AMBER CREWES

PEN-N-A-PAD PUBLISHING

Copyright © Pen-n-a-Pad Publishing

First published in August 2018

All characters and events in this publication, other than those clearly in the public domain, are fictitious and any resemblance to real persons, living or dead, is purely coincidental.

Copyright © Pen-n-a-Pad Publishing

The moral right of the author has been asserted.

All rights reserved. This book or any portion thereof may not be reproduced or used in any manner whatsoever without the express written permission of the publisher except for the use of brief quotations in a book review.

For questions and comments about this book, please contact
info@ambercrewes.com

ISBN: 9781098909734
Imprint: Independently Published

OTHER BOOKS IN THE SANDY BAY SERIES

Apple Pie and Trouble
Brownies and Dark Shadows
Cookies and Buried Secrets
Donuts and Disaster
Éclairs and Lethal Layers

A SANDY BAY COZY MYSTERY

BOOK FOUR

1

"It's a huge promotion!" Jack Irvin exclaimed as Meghan Truman beamed back at him. The pair stood in the dining area of *Truly Sweet*, Meghan's bakery, and Meghan could hardly believe Jack's good news.

"Being moved up from a police officer to a detective is serious business, and I can't believe it just happened to me." Jack explained, his face filled with pride.

Meghan could see the excitement in Jack's blue eyes, and she felt butterflies in her stomach as he grinned at her. She could hardly contain her crush on Jack; they had been on several dates together over the last few weeks, and as she stared up at his enormous smile and deep dimples, Meghan hoped she wasn't blushing *too* hard.

"I'm so excited for you," she said. "This is cause for celebration. How about I bake a nice black forest cake for you? You could take it in to work to celebrate. I'm sure the folks at the station would love some treats."

Jack nodded enthusiastically. "That's *truly sweet* of you to offer," he replied, winking at Meghan as the heat rose to her cheeks. "I love your cakes so much, but you know what would be great, Meghan? Donuts!"

Meghan's dark eyes widened. "Donuts?" she answered weakly. "Are you sure?"

Jack bobbed his head affirmatively. "Yeah! Chief Nunan was just talking about how badly she wanted donuts, and this is the perfect occasion. I know that cakes, pies, and cookies are your specialty here at the bakery, but could you swing some homemade donuts for me? That would be so awesome."

Meghan brushed a stray dark hair from her forehead and wrinkled her nose. "Come on, Jack! Let me make some brownies for you, or even a pie! Isn't it a big cliché for police officers to love donuts?"

"Guilty as charged! I'm just a big cliché, but humor me here, Meghan. Pretty please make some donuts for me? Please? I would be the most popular officer at the station if I walked in with some homemade donuts."

Meghan forced herself to smile. She ran a hand through her long, dark hair, and looked up at Jack. "Of course, *Detective* Irvin" she said, placing a hand on his shoulder. "I would be happy to make homemade donuts for you."

Jack gathered Meghan into a hug. "Thank you," he said. "You are truly the sweetest."

After Jack left, Meghan raced upstairs to retrieve her cell phone from the little apartment just above the bakery. She rifled through her purse, throwing aside gum wrappers, her sunglasses case, and her wallet. "Where is it?" she groaned, tossing the contents of her purse onto the wooden floor.

When she finally found her cell phone, she dialed the number of Karen Denton, one of her best friends. While at twenty-seven, Meghan was several decades younger than Karen, there had always been a strong connection between the two women, and whenever Meghan had any trouble, Karen was her first phone call.

"Come on, Karen, pick up!" Meghan muttered as the phone rang and rang.

Finally, Karen answered. "Meghan! How are you, sweetie?"

"Karen, I have a problem," she whispered, her stomach churning. "I need your help."

"What's that, sweetie? So sorry! I'm on mile fifteen of my twenty-mile run and the reception out here is just awful."

Meghan couldn't help but laugh. At seventy-three years old, Karen Denton was the fittest, healthiest person Meghan had ever known, and Karen was *always* training for something.

"My marathon is coming up next month, you know, and these back roads aren't going to run themselves! Meghan? Meghan? Are you there?" Karen asked, her voice cutting in and out. The call suddenly dropped, and all Meghan heard was the dial tone.

"Shoot," Meghan said. She thought for a moment, and then called Lori, her trusted assistant. Lori had been working as an assistant in the bakery for several months, and Meghan adored her company; Lori was like the little sister Meghan never had, and Meghan knew she could always rely on her.

"Meghan!" Lori squealed as she answered Meghan's call. "How are you?"

Meghan smiled. Lori was unfailingly friendly and energetic, and Meghan loved having her around.

"I have a little problem, Lori," she said, her voice serious. "Jack came over earlier and had something important to ask me…."

"Finally!" Lori exclaimed. "Finally! It's about time."

Meghan cocked her head to the side. "Finally? What are you talking about, Lori?"

"He came over and asked you to be his girlfriend! It's about time! You've been on a handful of dates with him, and even your dogs get along well together! I'm so happy to hear this news, Meghan! Jack is such a cutie. I can't believe he asked you to be his girlfriend at last."

Meghan sighed. She had been thinking a lot about their budding relationship; Meghan had moved to town and met Jack only a few months ago, and while she hadn't been fond of him at first, she had developed strong feelings for him. She *hoped* that perhaps someday, their relationship would turn into something more than just dates at the dog park and the occasional dinner together, but for now, she had bigger donuts to fry.

"That's not what he asked me, Lori," she said. "He asked if I could make donuts for him. *Donuts*, Lori!"

Lori paused. "Wait, what? I don't get it, Meghan."

Meghan took a long breath. "I don't know how to make donuts, Lori," her voice tinged with sadness. "I never trained formally to become a baker! I went to college, and then moved to Los Angeles to become an actress, and when that didn't work out, I ended up here in Sandy Bay."

"But your treats are *so* good, Meghan! Who cares about formal training? Lots of people don't train for things and are successful."

"Lori," Meghan said slowly. "You don't get it. I have *no idea* how to make donuts! I tried once, and it was a total failure! I couldn't get the filling right, I burned them in the fryer, and the sugar melted into a big mess when I tried to sprinkle it on top. I don't know what to do. I told Jack I would make him three dozen homemade donuts to celebrate his promotion at work, and I don't know how to make homemade donuts! What do I *do*?"

Lori giggled, and Meghan felt the sharp tug of rage in her

belly. "Lori!" Meghan exclaimed. "Why are you laughing at me? This is serious."

Lori giggled again. "I have good news for you, boss." Lori said. "When I was a little girl, my father taught me how to make donuts; it was one of our traditions, and each Saturday morning, we would spend time together making donuts for the whole family."

Meghan's spirits immediately lifted. "Lori, are you saying..."

"I'll help you, Meghan. You know I'll help you make the donuts for Jack. It's my pleasure, boss!"

The next two days were a flurry of activity in the bakery. Meghan waited on customers and filled her corporate orders, and Lori worked away on several types of homemade donuts. She and Meghan taste-tested each batch, and after making several hundred different donuts, the pair agreed on the best three flavors.

"My favorite is the toasted coconut mocha dream." Lori sighed as she bit into a warm donut.

Meghan nodded. "Yes," she said. "That's one of the best flavors. My two favorites were the blueberry lemon and the chocolate chai. I think we have some winners here, Lori. You have been such an angel to help me. Thank you so much for your help."

Lori blushed, her small, elfin face aglow with Meghan's compliment. "I was happy to do it, Meghan. Anything for you."

"We'll have to introduce these to our customers at the bakery, Lori. They're wonderful. You've been so helpful, and I want everyone in Sandy Bay to see how wonderful the donuts are."

Two days later, Meghan wanted to eat her words. Jack had been thrilled with the donuts; he raved about them to Meghan, and he even sent a thank-you card and a bouquet of red roses to the bakery. The residents of Sandy Bay had also been thrilled with the newest addition to the bakery, and after several hundred compliments, Lori's ego had exploded in a way Meghan had never experienced.

"They're saying *my* donuts are the *best* thing to happen to this town in years!" Lori bragged to Meghan as they loaded a tray of fresh donuts into one of the display cases. "Mrs. Sheridan told me she wishes that I had started baking them earlier. People are *begging* for my donuts. Begging!"

Meghan nodded politely. Lori's excitement over her success had been endearing at first, but after enduring Lori's endless boasting over the last few hours, Meghan was ready to scream.

"Kirsty Fisher told me that my donuts are so good that I should open my own shop. I knew my donuts were good, but now, I just *know* they're fantastic."

Meghan rolled her eyes. "Lori," she breathed. "I'm thankful you helped with the donuts; you really came through for me, and you know how much I appreciate your help! I just think that we should focus on work right now and maybe chat a bit less about the donuts? They were a great *team* effort, but we have a lot on our plate right now. Let's focus on the task at hand."

Lori narrowed her eyes at Meghan, and she angrily placed the tray of donuts on the counter beside her. "I knew it," Lori whispered. "I knew this would happen."

Meghan raised an eyebrow. "What, Lori?"

Lori frowned. "You're just jealous," she said. "Mrs. Sheridan said you would be jealous, and I can just tell. You're jealous that I made such amazing donuts, and that *everyone* is *obsessed* with them."

Meghan laughed aloud. "Lori, don't be silly," she said. "You helped make the donuts, but I created the flavors and picked the ingredients. This was a team effort, Lori. Let's not lose sight of that..."

Lori crossed her arms across her chest and glared at Meghan, her eyes flashing with anger. "A team effort? Meghan, come on. You may have helped, but I made these donuts with my own two hands. I have *so* much potential. Everyone in Sandy Bay has been telling me that after tasting *my* donuts. Don't kid yourself!"

Meghan stared at her assistant, her lips turning downward. "Lori," Meghan advised. "Please don't speak to me like that. I don't appreciate the attitude."

Lori tore off her yellow apron and threw it on the wooden floor in front of Meghan's feet. "Fine," Lori said. "I'll take my attitude somewhere else!"

Lori turned on her heel and stomped out of the bakery, slamming the door as she left. Meghan sighed. "That wasn't truly sweet of her, was it?" Meghan muttered to herself. She was familiar with the saying that all good things must come to an end, but she never in her wildest dreams foresaw her relationship with Lori ending this way.

2

"And then she walked out! It was so rude, Karen. I've never seen Lori act like that. She's usually such a sweetie, and she was just awful to me!" Meghan later ranted to Karen on the telephone, feeling the frustration bubbling in her chest.

"She called me later to apologize, but it didn't feel very genuine; she mentioned that the courts have given her full access to her late father's estate, and she's thinking about selling their family business to attend college. I just don't know how invested she is in *my* business anymore, Karen! Her little show today at the bakery was too much, and such a hasty apology *didn't* feel nice, either."

Karen sighed. "Pride can make the prettiest girl ugly," she replied. "I remember when I won my first triathlon. I broke a Sandy Bay record that had been standing for over fifty years, but Meghan, that victory made me too big for my britches. I marched around this town for *days* with my head held higher than a queen. Looking back, I wish I had been more humble, but like little Lori, I was just a young, naive girl. I didn't understand how silly I made myself look."

Meghan groaned. "I just want things to go back to normal, Karen! Lori has been such a good assistant to me, and while I love having the donuts in the bakery, I don't want any more trouble between the two of us. I just want things to be relaxed and easy again."

"Well," Karen said. "You said Lori offered an apology earlier. I know you weren't pleased with it, but sweetie, I think you're going to have to accept it, at least for your own sanity. The girl lost her way for a day or two, but Lori isn't a bad person. It sounds like she's just happy to have something to be proud of. She hasn't had it easy, that Lori, and I'm even *glad* that she had the opportunity to do something big."

Meghan took a long, deep breath. "You're right, as always," she said to Karen. "I know it's been difficult for Lori; her father was never nice to her, and when he died unexpectedly, I know she was very upset. I'm glad she's had something of her own to smile about with those donuts of hers."

"Fabulous! That's the spirit!" Karen cheered. "That's my Meghan. Just be patient and kind with her, and everything will work out. Just let Lori do her thing, Meghan, and eventually, it will all work out. I know you, and I know Lori, and I *know* that the two of you will be *fine* come tomorrow."

Karen could not have been more mistaken. The next morning, Lori sauntered into the bakery, her chin tilted upward as she strolled inside.

"Hey, Lori!" Meghan said cheerfully, hoping their day would be less eventful. "How's it going?"

Lori smoothed down her pixie cut and sashayed across the wooden floor, her hips swaying and her shoulders moving in sync. "Oh, hey," Lori said dismissively. "'Sup?"

Meghan pursed her lips. "Sup? Umm?"

Lori rolled her eyes. "It's a way of saying 'what's up'."

Meghan nodded. "Yeah, I know. Anyway, how are you? All okay, today?"

Lori flashed a brilliant smile at Meghan and daintily sat down at one of the white iron tables in the dining area. "We need to talk, Meghan," Lori said matter-of-factly. "Have a seat."

Meghan slowly lowered herself into one of the little white chairs, annoyed that Lori was inviting her to sit in *her* own bakery. "Okay?"

"Look," Lori said, leaning back into her chair and draping one leg over the other. "It's been fun to work here, Meghan, but after everything this week, I just don't know about my future at Truly Sweet."

Meghan inhaled through her nose and exhaled through her mouth, willing herself to remain calm. "What do you mean, Lori? I thought things were okay between us? You called yesterday and apologized for your outburst, and I accepted your apology. I thought we were good?"

Lori rolled her eyes and gave Meghan a pitying look. "Meghan," Lori said. "I've done a lot of thinking, and if I sell my father's business, I won't really need this job anymore. So many people have been complimenting my donuts and talking to me about my potential, and I just think I have more to offer than the average person! I think I can do amazing things, and I just don't think amazing things can be done *here*."

Meghan bit her bottom lip, feelings of rage and hurt swelling in her chest. She was immensely proud of her bakery; Meghan had built Truly Sweet from the ground up, and it was one of the most successful bakeries in all the Pacific Northwest! Lori's attitude was hurtful, and Meghan fought back tears as she looked Lori in the eye.

"I'm sorry you feel that way," she said flatly. "What are your plans, then?"

"I want to duck out of Truly Sweet in two weeks," Lori

informed Meghan. "I think I can be great somewhere else, *or* on my own."

Meghan nodded. "Fine," she whispered. "I guess I'll consider this your official two weeks' notice?"

Lori nodded emphatically. "Yep. This is it. Well, I had a week of vacation time saved up too, so I want to take that next week. Friday is really my last day here. I just wanted to let you know."

Meghan stared at Lori, clenching her hands into fists under the table. "So you have three days left here. Got it. Thanks for letting me know, I guess..."

Lori shrugged. "You're welcome. I guess we should get to work now. I saw the order sheet in the back when I came in, and we have a few hundred donuts to make. I guess I should show you how to make them yourself since I'll be gone after Friday, right?"

Meghan gritted her teeth. "Right," she said. "Let's get to work, Lori. Like you said, we have several hundred donuts to make, and I guess I'll be making them all by myself come next week..."

3

The next morning, Meghan awoke to three missed calls from Lori. She glared at the phone as she opened her voicemails, still angry from Lori's unexpected departure the day before. Meghan took a long breath, but before she could listen to the messages, Lori called again. Meghan answered on the second ring.

"Lori," Meghan said coldly. "What can I do for you today?"

Meghan was shocked to hear sobbing on the other end of the phone. Lori was crying, and Meghan could hardly understand Lori's words between the loud, heaving gasps.

"Lori! What's the matter?" she said, her frustration with Lori dissipating with every wail she heard.

"I'm embarrassed, Meghan. I was terrible to you yesterday. I had a big head from everyone saying such nice things to me, and I treated you horribly. I'm so sorry."

Meghan's heart warmed as Lori continued. "My whole life, I worked for my father. He never believed in me, and he never let me go after my dreams. I was just expected to work for him in that tea shop forever. Now that he's dead, things have changed. *I* have changed, and when people started paying attention to me, it just felt so good."

"Lori," Meghan said softly. "Lori, I forgive you. We all have big heads sometimes, and I know how easy it can be to let a kind word bring out the worst! Let's just put it behind us, Lori. Why don't you come in to Truly Sweet at noon? We can chat over some tea, and then we can get back to work! That new corporate order isn't going to fill itself."

Lori paused, and Meghan heard a loud, wet sniffle. "Lori?"

"I'm sorry for the way I acted, Meghan," Lori said gingerly. "I'm sorry about the way I treated you, but I meant it when I said I wanted to put in my notice at Truly Sweet."

Meghan's jaw dropped. "Lori, why don't you come on over? Let's chat about this in person."

Lori arrived at the bakery ten minutes later, and Meghan saw the concerned look on her small, delicate face. Her eyes were red and swollen, and her short hair looked unkempt.

"Let's sit down," Meghan said as Lori walked through the yellow door. "I'll get a treat for you. You look like you need a boost."

The two women sat down at one of the little white tables, and Lori buried her face in her hands. "I'm sorry, Meghan," Lori said. "I was so rude."

Meghan put an arm around Lori's shoulder. "I told you, Lori, it's fine. I forgive you. We all mess up. Don't sweat it. I want to talk about the last thing you told me. Do you really want to leave Truly Sweet? You are a *great* assistant, Lori. You have real talent in the kitchen. I like having you around, and I would be sorry to see you go."

Lori slowly raised her head, but she did not look Meghan in the eyes. "I'm sure," Lori whispered.

Meghan nodded. "Okay," she said slowly. "That's your choice, of course. Can I ask why, though, Lori? I told you that

I forgive you. We're good, Lori. You and I are fine! What makes you want to leave Truly Sweet?"

Lori wiped a tear from her pale face. "After everyone started complimenting my donuts, I started thinking," Lori explained. "It felt so good to get that praise, and I thought about all the things I haven't done yet that I would like to be praised for someday. Meghan, my dream was always to be an architect. I never told my parents; I knew there wasn't enough money to send me to some fancy college, and I didn't want to make them sad by asking. But now... my father is gone, Meghan. His tea shop is sitting empty, and I'm thinking about selling it. I could make enough money to pay for college. I could finally live *my* dreams, Meghan!"

Meghan's eyes widened. "Have you spoken to anyone about this? This is a big decision, Lori."

Lori smiled. "I called Kayley Kane, the real estate agent. I used to babysit for her kids before she and her husband got divorced! Anyway, Kayley is really nice, and she thinks if I want to sell, the time is now. She said that I could get a good price for the shop, but if I sit on it, I might lose out."

Meghan rested her elbows on the table and folded her hands neatly in front of her. "So let me get this straight," she said down-to-earth. "Your plan is to sell the tea shop quickly and then start college?"

Lori nodded. "Exactly! That's what I want to do, Meghan. I think the time is right, and Kayley swears that I can get at least enough money to pay for a full three years of college. Three whole years, Meghan!"

Meghan saw the hope in Lori's large eyes. She reached over and took Lori's hands, squeezing them in her own. "I didn't even know you had these dreams, Lori," Meghan confessed, looking into Lori's face. "I feel like a bad friend for not knowing this about you."

Lori shook her head. "No one knew, Meghan. You're a

good friend! A wonderful friend! It's been such a fun time working at Truly Sweet, and I hope there are no hard feeling between us."

Meghan smiled. "Of course not, Lori. We're good. I'm happy to see you do something that makes you happy, and if you feel like this is the right path, then I support you. Is there anything I can do for you? Do you need any help from me? You're making a lot of big decisions right now, and if you need me, I'm here for you."

Lori's eyes brimmed with tears, and she hiccupped as she leaned over to embrace Meghan. "You are the best, Meghan," Lori said. "You are the nicest person I know. I'm lucky to have you."

Meghan hugged Lori tightly. "Seriously! Do you need anything? I'm happy to help."

Lori pulled back and nodded. "I do have a lot on my plate," Lori admitted. "Kayley is coming by tomorrow to take photos to help sell the tea shop, and the place needs to be spotless! Any chance you could help me clean for a few hours? I don't know how I am going to do it all by myself."

Meghan rolled her eyes. "You are so silly," she said. "You've helped me with so much. Of *course* I'll help you clean up the tea shop. It would be my pleasure."

Lori shrieked. "Hooray! You are the best."

Meghan grinned. "I'm just glad you're so happy. I think your biggest adventures are yet to come, Lori! Whatever is around the corner for you is going to be *big*. I just *know* it."

As the two women hugged again, the little silver bells attached to the front door of the bakery chimed. Meghan dismissed the sound; customers came in and out of the bakery all the time, and she was used to the tinkling of the little bells. She watched as Lori's eyes widened; Lori was facing the door, and Meghan pulled back in concern.

"What's the matter? Are you okay?"

The color drained from Lori's face, and she started to shake. A stocky, dark-haired man stormed over to the table, his blue eyes narrowed. He tossed a bouquet of flowers on the table in front of Lori and glared.

"Welcome to Truly Sweet! Can I help you?" Meghan asked the man, looking to Lori for an explanation.

"Uncle Felix," Lori said weakly as the man scowled.

"They told me I would find you here, little niece," the man addressed Lori. "And over my dead body are you going to sell *my* brother's tea shop."

4

"It was so awkward," Meghan said to Jack as they walked their dogs along the beach. "Lori hadn't seen her uncle in *years*, and he just arrived out of nowhere! He didn't bother to come to attend her father's funeral, and now, he's demanding she keep the tea shop open."

Meghan and Jack strolled slowly along the pebbly beach as Dash, Fiesta, and Siesta frolicked through the waves. It was a chilly day; the wind from the Pacific Ocean had been cutting through Meghan's thin jacket, but upon seeing her shivering, Jack had given her his thick, wool sweater to wear. Meghan liked the texture and pattern of the sweater, but what she liked most was Jack's attention; he had immediately noticed how cold she was, and now, she reveled in the soft sweater that smelled just like him.

"That is crazy," he said, looking out over the water as the sun slowly floated down toward the horizon. "What else did he say?"

"He told Lori he was ashamed of her for tarnishing her father's legacy and then scolded Lori for working in a 'second rate sweet shop'!"

Jack scowled. "Lori's father didn't have a legacy," he said. "Well, at least not a good one! Everyone in Sandy Bay knew Norman was a jerk. He was mean to Lori, he was a jerk to his customers, and his tea shop was just okay. I don't understand what this guy's issue is."

Meghan continued. "This morning, he and his wife, Lori's aunt Becky, came back by the bakery. Lori was there picking up her last check from me, and the pair of them were nasty *again*."

Jack shook his head. "I don't get it," he said. "What do they want from Lori? Her father is dead, and she doesn't want to run a tea shop by herself. Why do they have a problem with that? Why are they coming out of the woodwork *now*?"

Meghan shrugged. "I don't know, *Detective* Irvin," she teased. "But it *does* seem fishy to me. Maybe you should watch out for them. You *are* the town detective now."

Jack grinned. "That's right, Ms. Truman. It's my job to watch out for this town, and everyone in it, including *you*."

Jack looked down at Meghan and smiled. She beamed up at him, and he leaned down toward her. He put a hand on her arm, and slowly, his body drew closer to hers.

"He's going to kiss me!" Meghan thought to herself, closing her eyes in preparation for the moment she had been looking forward to for weeks. She tilted her chin upward, but nothing happened. Suddenly, Jack removed his hand from her arm, and she opened her eyes.

"Hey!" Jack shouted, turning as his dog, Dash, began to bark. "Dash! Hush! You're fine."

Dash kept barking, and Fiesta and Siesta joined in. The three dogs ran out of the waves and across the beach.

"Dash, *come*!" Jack yelled sternly. "Dash!"

Dash did not obey Jack, and the dog began running away. Fiesta and Siesta watched as Dash sprinted down the beach, and they joined him, their small legs moving quickly across the dark sand.

"Hey!" he called out. "Dash! *Come!*"

Meghan laughed. "I don't think he's going to follow your orders, Detective," she said playfully. "Come on. Let's go chase down our dogs."

Early the next morning, just as Meghan unlocked the front door of the bakery, Felix Butcher burst through the door.

"Good morning, Felix," Meghan said through gritted teeth. This was his third visit to the bakery, and as their first two encounters had been terribly unpleasant, Meghan was not pleased to see him. "Can I help you with something?"

Felix crossed his arms and glared at Meghan. "Where's Lori? Becky and I need to speak to her again, and she isn't at home. I figured she'd be here."

Meghan shook her head. "I haven't seen her yet today," she said politely. "May I take a message?"

Felix cleared his throat and stuck out his chest, drawing himself to full height and making Meghan feel small. "Look," he said, looking down at Meghan. "Lori and I have some business to talk about, and I need to get in touch with her. Are you *sure* you don't know where she is?"

Annoyed at Felix's imposition, Meghan stood on her tiptoes and looked him straight in the eyes. "She isn't here," she said firmly. "She isn't here, and I don't think you have business with her. I heard her tell you twice now that she is selling the tea shop. She is an adult woman, and if she wants to sell it, I don't think it's your business."

Felix laughed, raising a dark eyebrow in amusement. "Well, look at you. A tough girl, I see! Well, it's cute that you're speaking for Lori, but I won't have it. She isn't selling, and that's that."

Before Meghan could reply, a loud scream rang through

the bakery. Meghan glanced at the door. Sally Sheridan, one of Sandy Bay's oldest residents, was standing in the doorway, her eyes wide, and her hands clasped to her cheeks.

"It's a ghost!" Mrs. Sheridan howled, pointing at Felix. "It's the ghost of Norman Butcher! Ms. Truman! I came here to return these nasty donuts and ask for a refund, and I find *this*? Do you see that you have a *ghost* in your bakery?"

Mrs. Sheridan hobbled towards Meghan and Felix, her wooden cane raised high above her head. She reached out the cane and waved it at Felix. "Be gone, ghost! Be gone!" The cane struck Felix on the forehead, and he stumbled backward into one of the little white tables.

"Mrs. Sheridan!" Meghan cried. "Stop! Stop, Mrs. Sheridan."

"Ghost, be gone! Be gone, Ghost!" Mrs. Sheridan screeched, beating Felix on the head with her cane. "Be gone!"

"Hey, lady! Stop it! What are you doing?" Felix yelled. "Cut it out, lady."

Mrs. Sheridan raised her cane over her head, but before she could bring it down on Felix's head once again, a hand reached for her arm.

"Stop it, lady!"

Felix, Meghan, and Mrs. Sheridan turned to find Becky, Felix's wife. "What do you think you're doing to *my* husband?"

Mrs. Sheridan's eyes widened, and a look of confusion crossed her wrinkled face. "Young lady!" Mrs. Sheridan lectured Becky. "This is a *ghost*! This apparition is the ghost of Norman Butcher, young lady. This terrible bakery not only has bad food, but it has *ghosts*! I'm trying to make this one leave. Give me my cane back so I can get rid of him!"

Becky threw the cane across the room. "That is my

husband, *Felix* Butcher, you old bat! He is Norman's *brother*! He isn't a ghost."

Mrs. Sheridan bared her teeth and clenched her fists. "*Now* you tell me? Ms. Truman! Why did you let me exert that much energy if this fellow isn't a ghost! Shame on you, Ms. Truman, for letting me believe this fellow was a ghost. I am leaving, and I will be back for my refund later. This place is just shameful. A terrible place!"

Mrs. Sheridan walked across the room to retrieve her cane. She shot a look of disgust to Meghan as she left, and Meghan sighed in relief as the chime of the little silver bells signaled Mrs. Sheridan's exit.

"Now then," Meghan said, looking at both Becky and Felix. "What do you two need? I don't know where Lori is, nor do I think you two should be bothering her."

Becky glared at Meghan. She would have been a pretty woman, but her lined face and graying hair took away from her looks, and Meghan noted the sinister look in her eyes.

"Look, little girl," Becky said, pointing a finger at Meghan's chest. "We're here for business, and our business is *none* of your business."

Felix nodded. "Don't think you're going to stand in our way," he said. "My brother's tea shop isn't closing, and that's the end of the story. It's none of your business, and if you think you're going to talk Lori out of anything, you're *dead* wrong."

Meghan felt her heart beat faster in her chest. She reached into her pocket and fingered her cell phone. She wondered if she could discreetly call Jack; Felix and Becky were making her feel uncomfortable, and Meghan felt as though she needed backup.

"Hey," a deep voice called as the little silver bells chimed from the doorway. Meghan looked up to see Jamie, the town handyman. She instantly felt relieved.

"Jamie!" Meghan cried out. "Good to see you!"

Jamie walked over to Meghan, his face dark. "What's going on, Meghan?"

Meghan gestured at Becky and Felix. "I think these people need to be escorted out of the bakery," she said, thankful that strong, tough Jamie had shown up at the right time. "Can you help me?"

Jamie nodded. "I'll take care of it, Meghan," he said. "You've helped me out before, and I'm real pleased to help you."

Jamie rolled up his sleeves to reveal his tanned, muscular arms. Becky shrank back from Jamie, but Felix didn't move. "Do I need to carry you two out?" Jamie challenged Felix and Becky. "The lady wants you to go, and you're both going to go *now*."

Meghan watched as Felix glared at Jamie. The two men were the same height, but Felix was no match for Jamie's thick, strong body.

"Let's go," Jamie growled, and he ushered Felix and Becky out of the bakery. "You two stay away from Meghan and her bakery. If I hear you're bothering her, or anyone else in this town again, you'll be answering to *me*."

5

Meghan's eyes widened as Jamie walked out with Becky and Felix. She felt her shoulders instantly relax as she watched them turn the corner, and she wiped the sweat from her brow.

"Ugh," she said to herself as Jamie walked back through the door. "Thank you, Jamie. I'm so glad you were here. They creep me out, and I'm thankful for your help."

Jamie nodded, adjusting the strap of his dirty overalls and giving Meghan a kind smile. "No problem, Meghan. I was just in the mood for something sweet, and one of your cookies sounded real nice. I'm glad I could help get those hooligans out of your place."

Meghan walked to the counter and retrieved a fresh oatmeal raisin cookie from the display case. "Here!" Meghan said as she handed the cookie to Jamie. "On the house."

Jamie smiled. "Awww, Meghan. That's too nice. Let me pay you."

Meghan shook her head. "No, no! You helped me out. I don't know what kind of trouble those two were looking for, but if it hadn't been for you, who knows what could have happened."

Jamie's face was solemn as he bit into the cookie. "Yeah," he agreed. "Who knows what could have happened."

Early the next morning, Lori burst into the bakery, her hair messy and her eyes bright. "Meghan! I need your help!" Lori exclaimed.

Meghan took a long, slow breath. She was happy to help Lori; she felt a deep sense of sisterly obligation toward the girl, especially after all the trouble with Lori's uncle, but Meghan was hesitant to get wrapped up in whatever storm seemed to be brewing at the tea shop. Only days after arriving in Sandy Bay, Meghan's name and reputation had been caught up in a murder scandal involving Lori's own father, and Meghan had nearly lost her business! Meghan's name had eventually been cleared, but after a few more obstacles in her first few months in Sandy Bay, Meghan wanted to lie low. Truly Sweet was surpassing its business milestones, Meghan and Jack seemed to be inching toward *something* special, and Meghan did not want to jeopardize her growing happiness with *another* scandal.

"Meghan? Can you help me?" Lori asked.

"What's up, Lori?" Meghan said hesitantly. "I have a lot going on today. Can this wait?"

Lori's eyes grew large with hurt. "Oh," she said, running a hand through her short hair. "I guess. It's fine. I can just ask someone else."

Lori turned toward the door, her shoulders slumped and her eyes cast downward. Meghan felt her heart lurch, and she reached for Lori's arm. "Wait," she said. "Just tell me what you need. I'll help you."

Lori's face brightened. "Can you come over?" Lori asked. "Kayley Kane is on her way over right now with a potential buyer for the tea shop! I'm not great at business and all of that stuff, and I need someone to talk to this buyer with me! Kayley is nice, but she makes me nervous. Will you come help, Meghan? Please?"

Meghan nodded. "Of course. Let me lock up, and then we'll head over there."

The two women arrived at the empty tea shop fifteen minutes later. Kayley Kane was waiting outside, tapping her pointed high heel shoes impatiently against the sidewalk. "Lori," Kayley said, clearly exasperated. "There you are!"

Lori smiled at Kayley. "Hi, Kayley! Thanks for coming over. When is the buyer coming?"

Kayley frowned. "The potential buyer is inside right now! You're late. What took you so long?"

Lori bit her bottom lip. "I'm sorry. I just needed some help. I brought my friend to talk to the buyer. Kayley, this is Meghan."

Kayley nodded sharply at Meghan. "Pleasure," she said to Meghan as Meghan extended her right hand. "But Lori, I'm your real estate agent. It's *my* job to talk to the buyer, got it?"

Lori nodded obediently. "Got it. So sorry."

Kayley reached into the pocket of her white pantsuit and revealed a small, golden tube of lipstick. She smeared a coat across her thin lips and then gestured at the front door. "Well, let's go. We've kept them waiting, and I don't want to be rude."

"See? She makes me nervous." Lori whispered to Meghan as the trio walked into the tea shop.

Inside, a short, raven-haired woman was examining the countertops. She was pale and harsh-looking, and she pursed her lips as she ran her small fingers delicately across the shelves and surfaces. "I think this will do," the woman said to Kayley. "There is a lot of work that needs to be done here, but I just *adore* the space! Where *is* the owner? I need to meet her in person before I can commit to making such a purchase."

Kayley pasted a smile on her face and shoved Lori forward. "This is the owner." Kayley said as the woman looked up at Lori. "Jacqueline, meet Lori. Lori's father ran the shop here, and now Lori controls the property."

Lori smiled warmly. "Nice to meet you, Jacqueline. What would you like to put in here? Another tea shop?"

Jacqueline shook her head. "No, no, no! There is a lot of work to be done here, but look at this lighting! Look at the aesthetic. Those high ceilings and tall windows just *scream* my vibe. This will be the perfect place for a salon. The ladies of Sandy Bay *need* a nice place to be pampered, and with some work, this will be perfect."

Kayley pulled out a clipboard from her large designer purse and showed it to Lori. "This is her offer, Lori. What do you think? She wants to sign *today*, and I think this is the perfect buyer for the space. You won't do much better than this."

Lori's jaw dropped as she studied the clipboard. "This looks amazing!"

Kayley smiled. "I think it's enough to send you to college twice over," Meghan heard Kayley whisper to Lori. "I think it would be best to sign now. We don't want you to lose out on this deal, Lori."

Lori grinned at Meghan. "Meghan! Did you hear Kayley? This will be enough to pay for college. This can all be over with today!" she exclaimed.

"What is going on here?"

The three women turned to see Felix stride through the front door of his late brother's tea shop.

"Oh no," Lori whimpered, reaching for Meghan's hand. "This can't be happening."

Felix growled at Meghan and Lori, but did not stop to

talk to them. He marched up to Jacqueline, who was looking at him in confusion. "Hey," he said, crossing his arms across his chest. "What do you think you're doing?"

Jacqueline leaned away from Felix. "I'm closing this deal," she explained politely. "I'm buying this space and turning it into a salon. Are you one of the owners or something?"

Felix nodded, but Lori shook her head. "No!" Lori cried out. "He isn't. Just ignore him, Jacqueline. He doesn't matter."

Felix turned to Lori. "Shut up. I *do* matter. This was my brother's shop, and I won't let it turn into some stupid salon, or anything else. I'm taking his business and restoring it to its former glory, and that is that, Lori."

Kayley cleared her throat loudly and glared at Felix, the clipboard still in her hands. She stepped in front of Lori and raised an eyebrow. "Excuse me," she said, placing her hands on her hips. "I'm in the middle of a sale, here, and you are interrupting my time. This is private property, and if you don't leave immediately, I will call the police."

Felix laughed in Kayley's face. "The police don't scare me, and I'm *family*," he declared. "You can't make me leave."

Kayley narrowed her eyes, looking steadily at Felix as the smile quickly vanished from his face. "The police don't scare me, either," she said quietly as Felix shifted uncomfortably. "Let's just say I have connections that would scare the police. You don't want to mess with me, or my connections. Now, get out of here, or I will have to make a call."

Felix's eyes widened, and he turned on his heel and stormed out. Kayley turned to Jacqueline, a thin smile on her face. "So sorry about that," she said, placing the clipboard next to Jacqueline. "This town has a few crazies, but he's harmless! Now, about the paperwork…"

Jacqueline shook her head and walked out of the shop, her body shaking. Kayley rolled her eyes.

"Lori," Kayley said, her voice filled with annoyance. "That

buyer is not coming back. Who was that guy, and what was his deal?"

Lori began to cry. "That was my uncle," she said, tears trickling down her face. "He doesn't want me to sell."

Kayley stared at Lori. "That was made clear," she said, snapping her gum and reaching for her phone. "Whatever his deal is, you need to take care of it. I can't sell this place if some creep is intimidating potential buyers, and I *need* to sell this place. My ex-husband has been sending less money for the kids lately, and I *need* this commission. Do you understand what I'm saying, Lori?"

The tears streamed down Lori's face. "I just wish he were dead like my father." she blubbered as Kayley shot her a look of disgust.

Meghan stepped forward. "She gets it," Meghan said to Kayley, seeing the hurt on Lori's face. "She'll take care of it."

Kayley nodded at Meghan and Lori and walked to the door. "Good. *Please* do."

Lori turned to look at Meghan as Kayley left. "This place *has* to sell," Lori said, her hands shaking. "I've waited too long to let another obstacle take me away from my dreams. I'm selling this place if it is the last thing I do, and I won't let *anyone* stop me!"

6

"It was just bizarre, Karen," Meghan said, sipping her chai latte as she and Karen caught up over breakfast at Truly Sweet. "The whole thing was strange. Felix and Becky are causing trouble, Kayley acted like she has mafia connections or something, and Lori is just losing it."

Karen shrugged, taking another sip of her protein shake. "I feel bad, sweetie," she said. "I promised you a quiet little small town, and Sandy Bay has been anything but."

Meghan sighed. "I'm getting used to it," she said, looking up as Jack's police car pulled up outside of the bakery. "At least some things are going well, though."

Karen grinned. "Look! He's coming in here," she said, gesturing at the door. "He's a cutie, that's for sure. How many dates have you two been on, now? Is he your boyfriend yet?"

Meghan shook her head. "No! I'm waiting for *something* to happen, but it feels like every time we get close to making things official, *something* happens. Like you said, this town has been anything but quiet lately, and it seems like we haven't had a chance to just relax."

Karen's eyes twinkled, and she leaned in toward Meghan.

"Well, that cutie is coming in right now. He has a serious look on his face. Maybe he's ready to ask you to be his girlfriend."

Meghan's stomach churned as Jack walked in. She ran a hand through her long hair, straightening her posture as Jack strode through the door. "Hey!" Meghan said, feeling herself blush as Jack approached the table. "We were just talking about you. In good taste, of course."

Jack's face was somber, and Meghan could see that he hadn't showered; his blonde hair was greasy, and his eyes were red. "Jack?" Meghan asked as Jack looked down at his shoes. "What's wrong? Are you okay?"

Jack shook his head. "There's been another murder, Meghan," he said. "Felix Butcher's body was found in the town center this morning."

Meghan gasped. *"What?"*

Jack nodded. "We've made an arrest. There was some significant evidence left next to the body, and we have a pretty clear idea of what we're dealing with, here. Or rather, who."

Meghan rose from the table. "Have you spoken to Lori yet?"

Jack sighed. "She's a mess," he informed Meghan. "She's out in my car right now. I went to tell her, and she had a total meltdown when I delivered the news. I have to take her to the station for some routine questioning, but she insisted I stop by here first to let you know what was going on."

Meghan turned on her heel and rushed outside to Jack's car. Lori was sitting in the front passenger seat, her head in her hands. "Lori!" Meghan called out as she opened the door. "Lori, I'm so sorry."

Lori wailed, her small body quaking. "He's dead, Meghan. He's dead, and they think Jamie did it."

Meghan's mouth dropped open in shock. "What? Jamie? He wouldn't hurt a fly, Lori. We all know that. He's all talk."

Lori shook her head. "They found bloody tools and overalls next to the body, and they belong to Felix! Someone heard him threatening Felix and Becky when he made them leave your shop, and that was enough for the police to arrest him."

Meghan frowned. "This doesn't make sense. Jamie is a good man. He wouldn't kill anyone."

Lori gasped for breath. "They found his stuff, Meghan," Lori cried. "There's no other explanation!"

Jack walked up behind Meghan and placed a hand on her shoulder. "Meghan," he said gently. "I need to take Lori down to the station. I'll call you later if there are any updates."

Meghan nodded. "Okay," she said to Jack. "Lori, I'm so sorry. Just try to breathe and relax. It will all be okay."

Lori did not respond; she was huddled in the passenger seat bawling, and Jack slowly closed the door. He squeezed Meghan's arm and then drove off. Meghan stood outside the bakery, her heart pounding in her chest as she heard the screech of sirens.

"How could this happen again?" Meghan asked herself. "*Another* murder in Sandy Bay?"

"Meghan? What on Earth is going on?" Meghan turned to find Karen behind her.

"Felix Butcher is dead, and they think Jamie did it." she explained, her face pale.

"What? Jamie? Jamie wouldn't hurt a fly." Karen insisted. "I've known him for years. He's a gentle giant. Why do they think Jamie did it?"

Meghan looked down at the ground, her eyes filled with sadness. "Lori told me they found things of his next to the body," she said. "They found a pair of his overalls and some of his tools. They were covered in blood."

Karen shook her head and folded her arms across her chest. "No," she said. "Meghan, *no*. You and I both know how easy it is for someone to be wrongfully blamed in this town. We aren't going to let some silly overalls and tools stand in the way of Jamie's innocence. We *must* look into this immediately."

Meghan bit her lip. "Karen," she whispered. "I don't know if I can do this again. I don't know if I can go through another scandal. Things are finally good for me here, and I think if I poke around in this kind of business, my name could get sullied again."

Karen narrowed her bright blue eyes at Meghan. "Meghan," she said sternly. "What if I had said that when *you* were falsely accused of murder? Without help, Jamie could be locked up for life! Looking into this is the right thing to do, and you know it."

Meghan sighed. "You're right," she admitted to Karen. "You're right."

Karen nodded. "Good girl. Now, let me call my personal trainer; we had a fifty-mile bike ride scheduled, but I can push that back to this evening. You and I are going to the station *right now*, and we are going to talk to Jamie."

7

"*I swear* it wasn't me," Jamie pleaded to Meghan and Karen as they sat across from him at the jail. "I didn't have anything to do with it! I didn't like that guy, or his wife, but I would *never* kill anyone."

Karen nodded sympathetically, but Meghan nervously peeked behind her at the door. Jack had begrudgingly snuck the women into an interview room at the police station, and Meghan was afraid that Chief Nunan, the police chief, would find them.

"Do you know *anything?*" Meghan asked, her heart pounding as she heard footsteps outside of the door to the interview room. "Your things were found next to the body, Jamie. How did they get there?"

Jamie shook his head and looked down at his feet. "Jamie?" Karen asked. "We know you didn't do it. Just help us help you!"

Jamie folded his hands and twiddled his thumbs. "It all started yesterday," he began, his scratchy voice shaking. "I was planting flowers near the town center, real close to where the late Mr. Butcher's tea shop was. That Felix fellow came around and started taunting me; he told me I would be planting flowers for *him* soon, and that *he* would be the owner of the tea shop soon. That made me mad, and I started shaking my fists at him. I remembered how nasty he was to you, Meghan, and I didn't want anything to do with him."

Karen leaned in toward Jamie. "Then what happened?"

Jamie sighed. "We started shouting at each other," he admitted, running a hand through his dirty hair. "He said some really nasty things to me, and he got in my face. I yelled some mean things back at him. Some folks walking around town saw and intervened… fortunately… I was so angry at him, and I walked on down to Winston's Bar and threw some back to settle my nerves."

Meghan's eyes widened. "So you had some drinks at Winston's? How late did you stay there?"

Jamie hung his head, his shoulders slumped. "I don't know," he said softly. "I drank an awful lot, Meghan. I don't do it often, but I was so mad at the bad fellow. All I remember from last night is walking into Winston's. This morning, I woke up to the police putting handcuffs on me in front of Mr. Butcher's tea shop. I don't remember anything in between."

Meghan raised an eyebrow. "So you don't remember *anything* between going into Winston's Bar last night and being arrested in front of Norman Butcher's tea shop this morning?"

Jamie buried his face in his hands and began to moan. "There, there, Jamie," Karen said soothingly, placing a hand on Jamie's back. "It's all going to be okay. We'll get to the bottom of this, I promise."

Jamie wiped his nose on his sleeve. "I didn't like the guy, but I would never kill anyone," he said as Jack slipped into the room.

"Karen, Meghan, that's all the time I can give you," Jack

said. "Chief Nunan is looking for Jamie, and I need to get you two out of here."

Karen nodded at Jack. "Thanks for letting us see him, dear," she said, her hand still on Jamie's back. "I've known him forever. Jamie is a good man, and Sandy Bay is lucky to have him."

Jack smiled weakly at Karen, but placed a pair of handcuffs on Jamie's hands. "Okay, Jamie," he said. "Let's get you back to your cell. Meghan? Would you wait for me in my office? I'll be down there in a few."

Ten minutes later, after Karen had bid Meghan farewell, Meghan greeted Jack in his office. "Hey," she said warmly. "How are you?"

Jack's face was dark. "I'm tired," he said. "It's been a hard day. I didn't expect this kind of mayhem during my first few days as a detective, and I honestly don't think Jamie did it."

Meghan took a long, deep breath. "Okay," she said slowly. "What makes you think that?"

Jack shrugged. "Gut instinct, although I have to admit the evidence against him is quite compelling. Felix was stabbed to death, but please don't share that; it isn't common knowledge yet, and I've already bent enough rules for you today."

Meghan bobbed her head in agreement. "My lips are sealed. So, if the evidence is compelling, what makes you think he didn't do it?"

"The facts are incriminating, but I don't think it was Jamie. The coroner's report states that whoever stabbed Felix was left-handed. Jamie is *right-handed*, Meghan...."

Meghan's dark eyes widened. "Then why is he still here, Jack? Why is he still in jail?"

Jack frowned. "It's complicated," he admitted. "Chief Nunan has ordered us to hold him until we find a better lead to suggest otherwise. With all the trouble this has caused,

Chief Nunan doesn't want to cause more of a stir in Sandy Bay, and this is just for the best."

"So you're telling me Jamie didn't do it? You know that for a fact?" Meghan asked, her voice hopeful.

"In my professional opinion, while his clothes and tools *were* found next to the body, I do not believe Jamie killed Felix."

Meghan's shoulders relaxed, but almost immediately, she sighed in frustration. "Jack," she said. "That's great and all; Jamie has always been kind to me, but the facts are the facts. His things were next to the body. Jack, if Jamie didn't kill Felix Butcher, *who* did?"

8

"But I'm just not ready, Kayley!" Meghan heard Lori shriek. "I'm not ready to talk about selling anymore. My uncle *just* died."

Meghan hastened her pace and burst into the tea shop to find Lori and Kayley glaring at each other. She stepped between the two women and held her hands up. "What is going on here?" she asked, seeing the fury in Lori's eyes.

"She just marched in here and demanded I sell the tea shop *today*," Lori said, pointing at Kayley. "I need more time to process everything that's happened with my uncle, and *she* won't leave me alone."

Kayley snapped her gum and studied Lori's frustrated face. "Look," Kayley said to Meghan. "I've been in this business awhile. I know what I'm doing. This tea shop's value is going to *plummet* if she doesn't get it together and let me make a deal."

Lori balled her hands into fists. "I just want a few days. That's all I want. She's being unreasonable, Meghan."

Kayley rolled her eyes. "I can't deal with this *child*," she said to Meghan as she gestured dismissively at Lori. "I've invested too much time and energy to get a great deal for you. I'm over these little games. I'm sorry your uncle died, but you need to get it together and help me help *you*."

Lori's eyes filled with tears. "Can't you just give me *one* more day?"

Kayley huffed, tossing her short, blunt brown bob behind her shoulders. "Fine," Kayley said, narrowing her eyes at Lori. "One more day, but after that, if you can't commit to making something work, I'm done."

Meghan and Lori watched as Kayley adjusted her purse and marched out the front door, and Lori wiped the tears from her cheeks as Meghan pulled her in for a hug. "Hey," Meghan said softly. "It's okay. We all need time to grieve, Lori, and if you need time, it's fine. Kayley is all talk, I can tell."

Lori shook her head. "No," she said. "Kayley Kane has always been a no-nonsense lady, but ever since her husband left, she is just *mean*. She was serious about giving me one more day, I can tell, and if she isn't helping me sell this place, I don't know how I'll get it done."

Meghan nodded sympathetically. "So you're still planning to sell?"

Lori smiled softly, her eyes still red. "It's hard to think about, but now that Felix is gone, I truly have no one in my way. I can sell this place, go to college, and start living the life I've always dreamed, Meghan. It's a hard time, but there is a bright side."

"Ladies!"

Meghan and Lori turned to see Kirsty Fisher standing in the doorway. Dressed in a matching violet sweater and skirt and wearing a string of pearls around her neck, Kirsty was the epitome of elegance. Meghan was intimidated by Kirsty; while the two women both ran established organizations in Sandy Bay, Kirsty exuded confidence and poise, and

Meghan, with her curvy frame and shy spirit, felt dull and childish next to her.

"Hi, Kirsty," Meghan said, plastering a smile on her face. "What are you doing here?"

Kirsty pursed her lips and reached for Lori, wrapping her toned, tanned arms around her. "I heard about the tragedy with your uncle and wanted to offer my condolences in person," Kirsty explained, delicately hugging Lori. "What a terrible thing. A murder. What a *scandal*!"

Meghan stifled an unkind thought as Kirsty gave Lori a pitying look; Kirsty's ex-husband had recently been found guilty in a murder scandal, and Meghan thought it was ironic that Kirsty was bringing up Felix's murder to Lori.

"Anyway, I just thought I would pop by. I saw Kayley Kane storm out of here. She's in some trouble, you know. Well, I shouldn't say anything, but as the President of the Parent Teacher Organization at Sandy Bay Preparatory Academy, she's been giving me a little headache lately."

Meghan raised an eyebrow. "What do you mean, Kirsty?"

Kirsty leaned in. "Well, a little bird told me that Ms. Kayley Kane is several months late on the tuition payments for her children. Several months! Can you imagine?"

Meghan wrinkled her nose. "What does that matter, Kirsty?"

Kirsty shook her head. "It doesn't, I guess. I was just not surprised to see her leaving here in a fussy way. She's a snippy one, that Kayley Kane. She's always been so pushy. Anyway, Lori, I'm sorry for your loss. Meghan, nice seeing you."

Kirsty kissed Meghan and Lori on both cheeks before turning on her heel and strutting out of the tea shop. Lori leaned against the counter and wiped her brow. "That Kirsty Fisher stresses me out," Lori said quietly. "I am *spent*, Meghan. Spent! I can't take one more stressful thing."

"Lori."

Meghan and Lori gasped in unison as Kayley marched back into the tea shop.

"Look, I thought about what you said," Kayley said. "I brought you the paperwork for the tea shop sale, but I'm willing to give you another week or so, if you need it. This has been a difficult time for you, and I'm sorry I was so rude."

Lori smiled as Kayley handed her a file of documents. "Thank you, Kayley. I'll do my best to get things in order and make it easy for you to help me sell this place. You've been a big help. Thank you so much."

Kayley nodded curtly, shooting Meghan a business-like smile. "Of course. Just be in touch, okay?"

Kayley said goodbye and walked out of the tea shop. Lori grinned. "That made my day!" Lori exclaimed as she hugged the file to her chest. "A little more time is just what I need."

Meghan's heart was beating rapidly in her chest, and she felt her body grow cold as she recounted Lori's second interaction with Kayley a few moments ago. Kayley had handed Lori the file with her *left* hand.

9

"Come on, pups! Fiesta, Siesta, let's go!" Meghan called to her beloved twin dogs as she attached their leashes to their collars. "It's a gorgeous day, and we have business to attend to!"

Meghan guided the dogs down the stairs and outside, breathing in the thick, salty air. "Ahhh," Meghan said to herself as she strolled toward downtown Sandy Bay. "What a nice day it has been."

Siesta and Fiesta walked in unison alongside Meghan. It was only steps to the city center, and Meghan reviewed her mission in her head. She could not shake the image of Kayley Kane handing Lori the paperwork with her left hand, and from what Jack had told her, the autopsy report stated that Felix's killer *had* to have been left-handed! Meghan needed to find out where Kayley was the night of the murder, and she was determined to get the answers she needed.

"Here, my babies!" Meghan said to the dogs as they arrived outside of Kayley's office. Meghan tied their leashes to a bike rack, straightened her hair, and marched into the office with her head held high. Meghan was greeted by a petite, curly-haired young woman sitting at a thin wooden desk.

"Hello! What can I do for you today?"

Meghan smiled warmly. "I'm looking for Kayley. Is she in?"

The curly-haired woman bit her bottom lip. "Did you have an appointment with her? Ms. Kane is currently out of town and unavailable."

Meghan cocked her head to the side. "Out of town, huh? Do you know when she'll be back?"

The woman shook her head. "I don't think she said. She left in somewhat of a hurry, but I can take a message for you."

Meghan waved her hand in front of her chest. "No," she said casually. "That's fine, I'll just catch her some other time."

Fifteen minutes later, Meghan, Fiesta, and Siesta were sitting in Jack's office at the police station. Meghan had rushed to the station to share the news with Jack, and she was relieved that he was available to see her immediately.

"You're telling me that Kayley Kane, someone who is *very* invested in the sale of that tea shop, is not only left-handed, but that she's skipped town?" Jack asked, his brows raised.

Meghan nodded emphatically. "Yes! Jack, I think it's her. I think she did it. I've heard she really needs that money, and Felix was standing in the way of her big sale."

Jack whistled. "Well, Ms. Truman," he said playfully. "You may have solved another case for this tired old detective. Look at you!"

Meghan smiled. "It's the least I can do," she said. "The sooner this is all over with, the better for Lori."

Jack agreed. "I'll have my team out to search for Kayley ASAP. In the meantime, you lay low, okay?"

Meghan nodded. "I will," she assured Jack.

As Meghan and the dogs walked home, Meghan struggled to keep the dogs on the sidewalk; Fiesta and Siesta were growing larger and larger each day, and they practically dragged Meghan along with them.

"Relax, pups!" Meghan hissed to the dogs as they pulled her forward. "Slow down!"

Siesta and Fiesta did not listen, and before Meghan could properly scold them, their leashes flew out of her hands.

"Fiesta! Siesta!" Meghan called as both dogs ran away from her. Meghan felt the hot tug of dread fill her stomach, and she took off running behind the dogs. "Come back, Fiesta! Come back, Siesta! Come back *right now!*"

Meghan could not keep up with the dogs, and they disappeared from her sight. She *could*, however, still hear their loud barks, and she ran in the direction of their familiar yelps.

"Pups!" Meghan yelled. "Pups!"

Meghan turned a corner and found Becky, Felix's wife, snuggling the dogs. They were licking her face, and Becky giggled as Siesta burrowed into her lap.

"Fiesta! Siesta!" Meghan said in relief.

"These sweet babies found me," Becky said, smiling at Meghan. "Sounds like they gave you a little scare."

"They did," Meghan agreed. "They're getting too big for me, and I couldn't keep hold of them."

Becky laughed. "This is the best thing to happen to me in *months*. I love dogs, and children, and anything little and sweet, really, but Felix never let me have them. Dogs and children, that is."

Meghan saw the sadness in Becky's eyes. "I'm sorry about your husband," she said. "I can't imagine what a shock it must be for you."

Becky nodded. "It's been hard," she said, burying her face in Fiesta's soft curls. "Felix was all I had. We were going to have a nice life here, too. He was going to run that tea shop, and I was going to finally stay in one place. We've been traveling around doing business for years, and all I wanted was to settle down here in Sandy Bay. Felix grew up here, you know, and he always talked about how pretty it was. I just wish he could enjoy it like I am."

Meghan felt her heart drop. Becky looked so lost and alone, and while Felix had caused quite a stir in town, now, Becky seemed harmless.

"Well, thanks for letting me love on your babies," Becky said wistfully as Meghan collected Fiesta and Siesta's leashes. "This made my day. Truly."

Meghan smiled at Becky. "Hey, what are you doing right now?"

Becky sighed. "Well, between running back and forth from my motel to the police station to help with the investigation, I haven't been doing much of anything. I haven't felt too welcomed here in Sandy Bay; you small town folks really stay close with your own, and I'm on the outside with this terrible murder."

Meghan tucked a loose hair behind her ear and reached a hand out to Becky. "Well, I'm not a small town gal," she said kindly. "I moved here from LA a few months ago, and I know what it feels like to be by yourself in a new place. Becky, how would you like to come chat over tea and treats with me at my bakery? You look like you could use something to sweeten your day, and I would love to have you."

Becky's face brightened. "That would be so nice," she said, smiling softly at Meghan. "Now *that* would make my day."

10

"This is such a nice place you have here," Becky said as she sipped her Earl Grey tea. "I'm so sorry that Felix and I came in here and caused such a ruckus. I hate trouble, but Felix seems… seemed to be drawn to it. I'm so sorry."

Meghan shook her head. "Don't you worry about it," she said gently. "It's all okay. Now, try a bite of *this*. This is one of our newest treats. These donuts were made by *your* niece, Lori. She's quite a good baker, and I've loved having her here."

Becky bit into the donut and shrieked. "This is wonderful! Oh, my goodness!"

Meghan laughed. "I think that's just what you needed."

Becky nodded in agreement. "I think it was too. It's been a hard time, Meghan. The last few years….well, life with Felix was never easy. We were so young when we got married, and looking back, we really never knew each other at all. He only really cared about his business, not me, and there were so many things that I never got to do. We just traveled around the country starting and *failing* businesses."

Meghan frowned. "That must have been so hard," she said softly. "What a difficult way to live."

Becky shook her head. "It was worth it when we were young," she said. "Felix was a hard man to love, but we had something huge in common."

"What was that?"

"Flowers," Becky dreamily replied. "He and I just *loved* flowers. We lived on a little plot of land outside of Montana for a year when we first married, and we grew the most beautiful garden together. We had gardenias, and sunflowers, and petunias that were the color of a Mediterranean sunset. Our garden was the most magical place I had ever seen."

Meghan smiled. "That does sound wonderful."

Becky looked down at her cup of tea. "It was wonderful, but it was over too quickly," she said. "Felix had a business idea, and even though I begged him to stay in Montana, with our beautiful garden, he refused. We moved to the middle of Sacramento, to a terrible little apartment in the middle of the city, and our garden was only a memory."

Meghan shook her head, studying Becky's face. "That's awful, Becky."

Becky sighed. "It was my fault for following him around. I had just hoped so badly that I could have a normal life here, with a normal job, like a teacher or something. With Felix gone, I just don't know what I'm going to do."

Meghan thought for a moment, but then her face lit up as she rose from her seat. "Becky!" she exclaimed. "Becky, I have an idea. Lori is leaving Truly Sweet to go back to school, and with all of my orders, I'll need some help around here. Why don't you stay in Sandy Bay and work for me? I've liked getting to know you, and the puppies already adore you. You could help in the kitchen, or with the customers. What do you think?"

Becky's eyes sparkled as she stood and hugged Meghan.

DONUTS AND DISASTER

"That is too sweet," she whispered into Meghan's ear. "Are you *sure*?"

Meghan gently pulled back and nodded. "Yes! I know how it feels to need a friend in this small town, and I feel like you could be a real asset here. You've done so many jobs, and I just know we'll find something here for you."

Becky grinned. "Felix always did say that my strudel was the best he ever tasted. Do you like German desserts? Those are my specialty!"

Meghan clapped her hands. "That's perfect! I'm always looking to diversify the menu, and you will be an excellent addition."

Becky wiped a tear from her eye. "This is the best news. Oh, Meghan! I've been so upset over Felix's death; our marriage wasn't the happiest, but he *was* my husband. I didn't have a plan or direction, and now, I can really settle down here."

Meghan beamed, thrilled to be helping Becky. Meghan was struck by Becky's troubled life with Felix, and she was eager to give her a chance; it wasn't easy to start over in Sandy Bay, but Meghan was confident that she could assist Becky, just as she had guided Lori. Suddenly, she heard music coming from outside of the bakery, and around the corner, the local ice cream truck appeared.

"Come on!" Meghan said to Becky as she took her by the hand and led her outside. "Let's get some ice cream. I know it's been a rough time for you, but this kind of news deserves a celebration."

Meghan and Becky walked to the back of the line outside of the ice cream truck. Meghan smiled at the families gathered in front of her, but her kind look was not returned. Even Milroy, the ice cream man, had a serious look on his face as he handed Meghan and Becky their ice cream cones.

"They seemed a little cold," Becky whispered to Meghan

as they walked back inside of the bakery. "I think these people don't like me. I know my husband's brother, Norman, wasn't the nicest, and that terrible handyman killed my husband... maybe this isn't the best place for me to stay, Meghan."

Meghan shook her head with vigor. "No! No, Becky. Don't take it personally. Trust me, it is hard for people in Sandy Bay to warm up to newcomers, but you'll fit in in no time. They'll *love* you here, I just know it."

11

"I can't believe you hired her, Meghan! She was *married* to my terrible uncle. She made a scene in here with him! What are you thinking?" Lori shouted as Meghan shrugged her shoulders.

"Lori, look," Meghan said. "Have you ever spent time with her? Becky is *sweet*. The dogs really warmed to her, and then we talked. Her life has been *hard*, and with what she's been through, especially with her husband being *murdered*, I think it is the right thing to do to offer her a job! I need the help, you know."

Lori scowled at Meghan. "You're just mad that I quit," she said accusingly. "You're mad that I quit, and you're sticking it to me by hiring that woman."

Meghan frowned. "Do you really think I would do that, Lori?"

Lori stuck her chin in the air and stomped out of the bakery. "I don't care what you do, Meghan! I'm not here, so it doesn't matter."

Meghan sighed as the door slammed behind Lori, but within seconds, the little silver bells chimed, and Jack walked into the bakery. "Meghan," he said, his eyes bright. "They needed someone to pick up the latest donut order, and I volunteered."

Meghan's annoyance at Lori instantly disappeared; she was happy to see Jack, and she thought he looked especially dashing in his new detective uniform.

"I'm glad you did," Meghan said, reaching under the counter to retrieve the box of fresh donuts. "This is a batch I made this morning. Lori showed me her tricks, and I think it's a good batch."

Jack grinned as he opened the box and reached for a donut, licking his lips as he ushered it to his lips. "Mmmhmmm," he groaned as he took a bite. "This is even better than the ones I've had before. You've outdone yourself, Truman!"

Meghan grinned. "Glad to hear it, Detective Irvin. So, how are you? How is the investigation?"

Jack sighed loudly. "It's not great," he said. "More tests have come back, and it's clear that Felix died from multiple stab wounds."

Meghan gasped. "That's terrible!"

Jack nodded. "Yeah, it's pretty horrible. Anyway, Jamie passed a polygraph test, so we are scheduled to let him go later tonight. It's pretty obvious that the tools and overalls were planted at the scene, so we don't have enough evidence to hold him, even if we wanted to. Our real suspect, Kayley Kane, is back in town, but we've had a hard time tracking her down to do an interview."

Meghan scowled. "Of course you have," she said. "I bet she's back to make sure Lori closes the deal, and then she'll take her money and run again."

Jack bit the inside of his cheek, and Meghan could see that he was weighing her words. "We're trying, Meghan. It's just a sticky situation through and through.

Meghan nodded. "I'm sure. I just hope you can get to

Kayley and get a confession out of her. She's a difficult woman!"

Jack rolled his eyes. "Oh, don't I know it," he said. "I grew up here, remember? Kayley Kane has always been a fighter, so I can't say any of this really surprises me."

Meghan and Jack chatted for a few more minutes. Meghan watched Jack as he told her more about the investigation, studying his handsome face. She also noticed his thick blonde hair; Jack's locks were the color of evening sunshine, and Meghan wanted nothing more than to run her hands through his mane. "Maybe someday," she thought to herself as Jack smiled down at her.

"Oh wait, excuse me, Meghan, but my cell is ringing," he said, holding up a finger to quiet Meghan. She listened as he whispered into his cell phone, seeing his expression change only seconds after answering the call.

"Okay, Chief Nunan," Jack said. "I'll be there in five."

Jack hung up the call and grinned at Meghan. "Well," he began. "I think we have her. Chief Nunan just called. She said that Kayley Kane was spotted in town and I need to join my colleagues to track her down. I need to go."

Meghan gave Jack two thumbs-up as he waved goodbye, and she wished him luck in finding Kayley. "Two-thumbs up?" Meghan muttered to herself as she watched Jack climb into his police car. "Why am I such a dork?"

Meghan sighed. She heard a whistle coming from the kitchen, and she raised an eyebrow in confusion. It was nearly nine in the evening, and the bakery had been closed for an hour.

"Hello?" Meghan called out, walking slowly into the kitchen.

"Meghan!" Becky cried out. "Hey! I thought I would get a head start on some of my strudel. I know I am supposed to start tomorrow, but I just wanted to get a jump on things! The recipe is complicated."

Meghan smiled warmly, happy to see Becky in good spirits. "That's so thoughtful of you, Becky," Meghan said. "Is there anything you need from me? I'm going to go upstairs soon and head to bed, but I can help for a bit now."

Becky nodded. "Sure! I would love some company. It was so nice chatting with you the other day. It's just nice to have some girl time, you know?"

Meghan grinned. "Absolutely! You'll have to have lunch with Karen Denton and me sometime. You'll just love her. Now, what can I do to help you with your strudel, Becky?"

Becky jerked her chin at the countertop beside Meghan. "Can you hand me that knife next to you, Meghan?"

Meghan reached for the knife and carefully placed it in Becky's outstretched hand. Becky smiled and turned back to the dough she had been kneading. She shifted her weight onto her left hip and moved the knife from her right hand to her left hand and began slicing the dough.

"She's left-handed," Meghan thought to herself as her body grew cold with fear. Becky cut the dough in long, calculated slices, and Meghan gasped.

"What's wrong?" Becky asked, placing her right hand on her hip and holding the knife in front of her. "Meghan? What's the matter? You look like you've seen a *ghost*."

12

Meghan shook her head as Becky held the knife in front of her. "It's nothing," Meghan said. "I'm fine."

Becky smiled and turned back to the dough. Meghan's hands shook as Becky sliced the dough with precision, and she struggled to maintain her composure.

"Just breathe," Meghan thought to herself as Becky contentedly cut the dough with the long, sharp knife. "Stay calm."

"Becky?" Meghan whispered, slowly backing away from Becky and the knife. "Becky, I know it's been so hard, and that your marriage wasn't the best, but you miss Felix, right?"

Becky kept cutting, her pace quickening as she nodded. "Sure," she said. "He could be a real jerk sometimes, but he was my husband. It's such a shame that he had to die like that. I still cannot believe that the terrible handyman stabbed him so many times."

Meghan's stomach lurched, and she stifled the urge to vomit on the kitchen floor. "Becky," Meghan said softly, still inching away from her. "How do you know that Felix was stabbed? That isn't common knowledge…."

Becky gripped the knife tightly in her left hand, turning to look Meghan in the eyes.

"What are you talking about, Meghan?" Becky said, her voice cracking as she said Meghan's name. "I think everyone knows that Felix was stabbed."

Meghan shook her head. "No one knows that," Meghan whispered. "That information hasn't been released to the public yet. Only one other person would know that Felix had been stabbed to death…"

Becky's eyes narrowed. "Excuse me?"

Meghan stared at Becky. "Only the killer would know that Felix had been stabbed to death, Becky…"

"What are you saying, Meghan?" Becky said flatly, her eyes dark.

Meghan inhaled sharply. "Becky… what did you do? What did you do to Felix?"

Becky raised an eyebrow. "What do you mean? I don't know what you mean."

Meghan took a long breath. "You *know* what I am asking you, Becky," Meghan said.

Becky rubbed the handle of the knife with her thumb, and Meghan felt a rush of nausea as the blade of the knife caught the light of the soft, pale lamp in the corner.

"Becky? What did you *do* to Felix?" Meghan asked again, swallowing the lump in her throat.

Becky rolled her eyes. "I didn't mean to kill him," she said. "But I can't say I'm too torn up about it. He was awful, Meghan! He bossed me around for years, and he made us look like fools everywhere we went."

"What happened, Becky?"

"The night he died, he begged me to come with him to the center of town. I was making something for dinner and he literally dragged me away from the kitchen. He wanted us to uproot the flowers that the handyman had planted; Felix said it would be revenge for that handyman talking down to us when he made us leave your bakery. I told him it was a bad idea, and we argued. He tried to hit me, and I waved my knife at him. It was self-defense, Meghan! I didn't realize I had stabbed him so many times. You have to understand."

Meghan shrugged. "So how did Jamie get caught up in this? You were trying to *help* him by stopping Felix from uprooting the flowers. Why did you make sure he got blamed?"

Becky frowned. "I didn't know what to do, Meghan! I was in shock. Felix was dead, and it was an accident, and I lost control. I came back in the morning to cover my tracks and saw that handyman passed out drunk nearby, and I just grabbed his things and left them by the body. I didn't know what else to do. You believe me, right? It was an accident."

Meghan nodded. "Of course," she said, reaching into her pocket for her cell phone. "It was an accident. You didn't know what to do."

Becky saw Meghan's hand in her pocket and grimaced. "Meghan," she said. "What are you doing?"

Meghan waved her hand. "Oh, nothing!"

Becky walked toward Meghan, pointing the knife at Meghan's chest. "You aren't going to tell anyone about this, Meghan. This is our little secret."

Meghan nodded, but turned on her heel to run. She dashed into the dining area, but tripped on her own feet as she rounded the corner.

"Come back here!" Becky screamed, lunging after Meghan, her face red. "Meghan! Come back here!"

Meghan stumbled to her feet and scrambled for the front door. She knew it was locked, but it would only take seconds to undo the latch, and if she could get herself out of the bakery, she could scream loud enough to attract the attention of passersby.

"Meghan!" Becky screeched as she dove across the dining area. "Meghan, just come back here. We'll talk about this!"

Meghan felt herself stumble, and she landed hard on the wooden floor. The fall knocked the air out of her, and she struggled to breathe. As she panted, Becky jumped on top of her. Becky straddled Meghan's middle, and she held the knife directly above Meghan's chest.

"Now," Becky said, grinning at Meghan. "Let's chat."

Meghan wheezed, trying with all of her might to regain normal breathing. Becky was crushing her, which didn't help, and Meghan was trying not to panic as her head began to spin.

"You've figured out my little secret, Meghan, and from the way you ran out, I don't think you're planning to *keep* my little secret, are you?"

Meghan choked as Becky shifted her weight. Becky slowly lowered the knife to Meghan's throat and gently traced the length of Meghan's neck with the knife's edge.

"I don't want to hurt you, Meghan," she whispered. "You were so sweet to me. I just can't let you go spoil my little secret. My life without Felix is just beginning, and I can't have *you* ending *my* new beginning. I'm sure you understand."

Meghan felt the tears well in her eyes as Becky smiled menacingly at her. As Meghan lay helpless on the hard, wooden floor, she thought of Fiesta and Siesta, her beloved dogs. She recounted her last encounter with Jack, and the harsh words Lori had spoken to her. She hoped that Lori could forgive herself for being so rude during their very last exchange. Meghan imagined Karen, who was probably out running or at the gym. Her heart swelled as she thought of her loved ones, but then, as she heard Becky's wicked laugh above her, her chest grew tight with fear.

"Goodbye, Meghan," Becky said. Meghan opened her eyes as Becky raised the knife above her head.

"So this is the end," Meghan thought, closing her eyes again as Becky brought the knife down for the final time.

Meghan heard the air shift as Becky brought the knife down, but before the blade could pierce her skin, a scream rang through the bakery.

"Stop that!" Lori shouted, running across the room and tackling Becky. "Get off of her, you witch."

The knife fell to the floor with a loud thud, and Lori entangled herself in Becky's limbs. The two women grunted and shrieked, and while for a moment, it looked like Becky was going to prevail over Lori, Lori took Becky by the hair.

"Stop it! Stop it!" Lori yelled, tugging hard on Becky's ponytail. "You're *done*! I knew you were trouble, just like my uncle. You're *done*!"

Meghan gasped as Lori rose to her feet and quickly reached for one of the little white iron chairs in the dining area. Lori held the chair above her head, and before Meghan knew it, Lori slammed the chair down on Becky's head. Becky moaned, but then, she was silent.

13

"I just can't believe it," Karen lamented as she and Meghan read through the Sandy Bay Gazette. Becky's mugshot was on the front page, and Meghan shuddered as she remembered their brawl only three days earlier. "I *knew* it wasn't Jamie who killed Felix, but his *wife*? How terrible. Who would have guessed? When you and I chatted after you offered her the job here, you just raved. I can't believe she turned out to be so vicious."

Meghan nodded solemnly. "I can't believe it, either," she said, hanging her head. "She fooled me, Karen. I still believe that her life with Felix was difficult, but I don't believe for a single second that the murder was an accident."

Karen shook her head. "There's no way, and the police don't believe it was an accident, either."

Meghan sighed. "I just feel terrible for how I jumped to conclusions about Kayley Kane," she admitted, pursing her lips as she recalled her harsh words against Kayley. "I was just adamant that *she* had killed Felix, and I was blind to Becky's ill-will. I just feel embarrassed."

Karen leaned in and wrapped her muscular arm around

Meghan's shoulder. "Hey," Karen said soothingly. "It was a mistake. You were worried about Lori, and you let that cloud your judgement. It was a learning experience, sweetie. It's over now. Don't beat yourself up too badly."

Just then, the silver bells chimed, and Lori walked into the bakery. "You will never believe what the police just uncovered about those people," Lori said breathlessly. "Felix and Becky had *felony* charges against them in five states! They were going to come here to swindle me out of the money from the tea shop, and then, they were planning to escape all the way to Qatar. Can you *believe* that? Thank goodness the police locked up that nasty bat of an aunt before she could escape."

Meghan nodded. "Yes," she said, remembering the sinister look in Becky's eyes as she dangled the knife above Meghan's neck. "I *can*. I don't know much about Felix, but Becky sure proved her true colors here."

Lori came to Meghan's side and wrapped her own arm around Meghan's other shoulder. The three women leaned against each other.

"Thank you for saving me," Meghan whispered to Lori. "You saved my life."

Lori shrugged. "I was coming back to apologize for being bratty. It was perfect timing, and I am so glad I found you before Becky hurt you."

Karen stood from her seat and kissed Meghan and Lori on their foreheads. "Girls, you two talk. I'm late for my lifting session with my trainer, but Meghan, let's catch up soon. Lori, you take good care, sweetie. Have a fabulous day, girls."

Karen waved goodbye, and Lori turned to face Meghan. "I have to tell you something," Lori said. "Kayley helped me sign off on the deal today. She tracked down Jacqueline, the salon owner Felix scared off, and Jacqueline is going to buy the property from me."

Meghan smiled at Lori. "That's great, Lori. I'm so happy for you."

Lori squeezed Meghan's hand. "I couldn't have done it without you, Meghan. You helped me by giving me a job at Truly Sweet, and you've supported me ever since. I'm going to chase my dreams at college, and it's really thanks to you."

Meghan shook her head. "No, Lori. Thank yourself. You are a strong, smart woman, and you made this happen. You should be proud of yourself. I know I am."

Lori hugged Meghan and said goodbye, leaving the bakery with an extra spring in her step. Meghan felt her heart swell as Lori walked away; when they had first met, Lori was sweet, but timid, and now, Lori was coming into her own at last. Meghan was happy for her friend, and she hoped that Lori would find what she was looking for when she started college in the fall.

"Meghan?"

Meghan looked up to see Jack standing in the door. She was thrilled to see him; in his new role as a detective, he had been managing the fallout from Becky's arrest, and Meghan had hardly spent any time with him in the last few days. Meghan smoothed down her hair and smiled.

"Jack," she said as he walked toward her. "How are you?"

Jack shook his head and pulled Meghan into a tight embrace. She could feel the heat of his body as she leaned into his muscular chest, and her stomach erupted into a parade of butterflies.

"How am I? No, Meghan. How are *you*? I'm so sorry it's taken me so long to get down here to check on you; this case spiraled, as you know, and I've been neck-deep in paperwork as I wrap up the investigation. Forgive me for not stealing away sooner."

Meghan breathed in the deep, masculine scent of Jack's

cologne, and she smiled. "It's fine," she said, pulling back and looking into Jack's blue eyes. "I'm fine, I promise."

Jack frowned. "I heard that she nearly killed you," he said. "I can hardly look at her, I'm so angry! If she had hurt you…."

Meghan waved her hands. "But she didn't. It's fine, Jack. Really, I'm okay."

Jack sighed. "You're a brave one, Truman," he said. "Now, come sit with me. There's something important I want to ask you."

Meghan's heart thudded in her chest, and she felt her stomach drop. Was Jack going to ask her to be his girlfriend?

"Meghan," Jack began as they sat across from each other at one of the little white tables. "This is an important question, and I think you are the best person I could ask to do this."

Meghan could hardly breathe; she lowered her eyes, and then she looked back up at Jack. She heard a yelp from the corner. Jack's dog, Dash, was playing with Fiesta and Siesta, but Meghan didn't peek over; her eyes were glued to Jack's.

"Yes, Jack? What can I do for you?" she asked, willing her hands not to shake.

Jack smiled. "Meghan, would you… teach me how to make homemade donuts? The folks at the station *love* them, and I want to try to make some of my own! What do you think? Can you teach me to be a truly sweet baker?"

Meghan's heart sank, but she forced herself to smile. Jack may not have asked her to be his girlfriend, but he *was* asking to spend more time with her. She took a long breath, and then nodded at Jack. "Of course," Meghan said. "I'd be happy to."

Jack beamed. "Great! How about right now? I have some ideas, too! There are so many flavors I want to try. I'm thinking a nice red velvet donut would be insane. Or maybe a strawberry frosted donut with sprinkles? What do you think, Meghan? Can you show an old dog like me some new tricks?"

Meghan looked at Jack's perfectly chiseled face, and she smiled even wider. "Yes," Meghan said. "I think we can figure something out together."

The End

AFTERWORD

Thank you for reading Donuts and Disaster. I really hope you enjoyed reading it as much as I had writing it!

If you have a minute, please consider leaving a review on Amazon, GoodReads and/or Bookbub.

Many thanks in advance for your support!

ECLAIRS AND LETHAL LAYERS

CHAPTER 1 SNEEK PEEK

ABOUT ECLAIRS AND LETHAL LAYERS

Released: September, 2018
Series: Book 5 – Sandy Bay Cozy Mystery Series
Standalone: Yes
Cliff-hanger: No

When a new girl comes to Sandy Bay with intentions to open a bakery, Meghan Truman is happy to share baking tips and some business advice. Things become awkward when this new girl steals not only her recipes and branding but also her biggest corporate order!

Her world is further thrown into a state of chaos when 'new girl' is found dead and her dearest friend is identified as the main suspect.

With so many conflicting clues pointing to different potential murderers, Meghan must slice through the layers of ambiguity shrouding this murder investigation and discover the real motive and culprit behind this heinous crime.

CHAPTER 1 SNEEK PEEK

If success had a taste, Meghan Truman was sure it'd taste like one of her desserts. Despite the many challenges her business had faced since its inception, she could confidently say it was a success, both in terms of the health of its finances and its reputation in the area. She was hopeful that her business would go from strength to strength, and she welcomed the challenge to exceed her customers' expectations.

It was a gray, windy morning, but she did not mind; while as a recent transplant from sunny Los Angeles, Meghan had not anticipated enjoying the weather of the Pacific Northwest, she found that the cool mornings and dark skies made her feel cozy and relaxed. She loved snuggling into thick, chunky sweaters and her knee-high boots, and in spite of the occasional rainstorm, Meghan felt more at home in Sandy Bay than she had ever felt in Los Angeles.

"It's a great day to be in Sandy Bay!" Meghan chirped to Fiesta and Siesta, her little twin dogs, as they playfully nipped at her heels as she prepared for the day. "The sun isn't shining, and from my window, the sea looks rough, but I can just tell that it's going to be a good day, my sweet puppers!"

Meghan smiled at her reflection in the mirror. Her dark, wavy hair was pulled back into a messy bun at the nape of her neck, and her deep brown eyes sparkled as she applied a layer of ballet pink lip gloss to her thick, bow-shaped lips. Meghan reached into her drawer to retrieve an apron, and she smoothed down the wrinkled front as she walked down the narrow staircase, both dogs following her as she entered the kitchen of Truly Sweet, her bakery.

The wind rattled the small, silvers bells attached to the front door of Truly Sweet, and she glanced up and smiled as a statuesque, curly-haired woman walked through the door. It was a quiet Tuesday morning, and the bakery had only been open for ten minutes, rendering Meghan pleasantly surprised to see someone stepping across the threshold of her shop.

"Good morning!" she chimed to the stranger as the woman approached the counter. Meghan could see that they were around the same age, and her smile widened; Karen, her dearest friend in her adopted hometown of Sandy Bay, was over seventy years old, and Meghan was eager to make some friends closer to her age; her former assistant, Lori, was close to her age, but had recently left for college, and Meghan brimmed with excitement as she studied the attractive young woman staring at her from across the counter.

"Hi," replied the woman, tucking a loose brunette lock behind her ear. "I'm Stephanie Cameron, and I'm new here to Sandy Bay. I've done some asking around; it's a small town, as you know, and everyone seems willing to give me every detail of every person in town. I hear that you're new to Sandy Bay as well?"

Meghan nodded enthusiastically. "I am." she responded

giddily. "My name is Meghan Truman, and I moved here a few months ago, so I know the lay of the land pretty well, but I'm not a native Sandy Bay-er. What brings you to town, Stephanie?"

Stephanie bit her lip and looked down at the wooden floor. "I'm from Indiana," she began. "My husband and I split up; I was an investment banker in Indianapolis and living the dream. But, some dreams come to an end…."

Meghan's lips turned down. "I'm so sorry to hear that," she said softly. "I'm sure Sandy Bay is very different than Indiana; I've never been, but I hear it's very flat there."

Stephanie nodded. "Very flat, and we have a lot of corn."

Meghan smiled. "We don't have a lot of corn here, but we have some gorgeous beaches, and the weather is just to die for! You can curl up with tea and a good book any day of the week, and it's always sweater weather in Sandy Bay."

Stephanie bit her lip. "That does sound nice," she said. "I'm hoping for a real change, and I think the Pacific Northwest is where I'll find it. I hope…."

Meghan nodded. "I hope Sandy Bay is the perfect place for you to have a fresh beginning. I came here from Los Angeles and didn't have a lot going for *me,* but *now…*" Meghan opened her arms to gesture at the counters and displays in the bakery. "Now, I have Truly Sweet, *and* some wonderful friends here."

Stephanie smiled at Meghan, showing one thick dimple etched into the side of her face. "That's actually what I came here to chat with you about."

Meghan cocked her head to the side. "Oh?"

Stephanie nodded. "I got into town a few weeks ago, and I've actually been thinking about starting my *own* bakery. I've done some research, and from what I've read, Sandy Bay is an ideal place to open a bakery."

Meghan grinned. "That's wonderful," she cried. "It's a truly sweet business to be in. I was *lost* until I started my business here, and I'm so excited that you'll have the same luck I did. Do you have any experience running a bakery?"

Stephanie shook her head. "No," she said quietly. "That's actually why I came to see you. I was at the grocery store last night, and when I chatted with the bag-boy, he mentioned that you were a nice girl with a new bakery. I just *had* to stop by and meet you. Can I ask you a huge favor?"

Meghan nodded. "I remember what it was like to be new in town," she answered, placing a hand on her heart and remembering the rocky beginning to her new life in Sandy Bay. "I'm happy to help. What can I do for you?"

Stephanie gestured at one of the little white iron tables in the corner. "Can we sit? Honestly, I want to pick your brain. I've always *dreamed* of starting my own bakery, but I don't know how to begin. I don't want to step on your toes; you seem like a nice girl, and I realize a new bakery would be competition, but do you think we could just chat a little about *your* experiences here in Sandy Bay?"

Meghan nodded. She had seen the hurt in Stephanie's eyes when Stephanie had mentioned her failed marriage, and Meghan knew how important it was to welcome newcomers to town.

"Absolutely!" Meghan exclaimed as Stephanie's eyes lit up. "Let me grab some treats for us; it's early, and I think some tea and fresh croissants would just be the coziest."

Ten minutes later, Meghan and Stephanie were laughing over the warm, soft croissants that Meghan had baked earlier that morning. Meghan leaned back in her chair, delighted to be advising Stephanie, who was proving to be good company.

"A bakery is like one of these croissants," Meghan giggled, licking her lips. "A bakery has many layers; there is the business layer of things, the merchandise, and the customers you have the pleasure to serve."

Stephanie smiled warmly. "That's a great way to think about it," she said, reaching over and patting Meghan on the hand. "It's been so kind of you to sit down with me about this; I was *so* nervous to come ask, but you've been such a dear."

Meghan beamed, her dark eyes shining. "I'm just happy that you're here. Sandy Bay is lovely, Stephanie; it's on the coast, the town is quiet, for the most part, and people here will embrace what you have to offer. I just know it!"

Stephanie nodded. "It's like you said, a bakery is about layers. That makes so much sense to me."

Meghan agreed. "If your customers know you, like you, and *trust* you, you'll get it right," she assured Stephanie. "With those layers, success is guaranteed!"

Stephanie glanced down at her watch, her eyes widening. "Oh, goodness! I have a meeting with my new finance guy in ten minutes. I'm sorry to cut this short, Meghan, but I'm so glad we got to chat."

Meghan rose to her feet and leaned in to hug Stephanie. "Don't be a stranger. Like I said, I'm always happy to help those who are new in town. Swing by anytime you'd like."

Stephanie waved as she walked out of the bakery and into the sunny morning. "I will! Thanks, Meghan!"

Meghan sighed happily as the little silver bells attached to the front door of the bakery chimed as Stephanie left. "There was my good deed for the day, and it isn't even ten in the morning yet" she laughed to herself, running a hand through her long, dark hair and adjusting the white apron around her waist. "She seemed like a great girl. I hope I didn't tell her too much, though; maybe she had a point about being competition to *my* bakery."

***

You can order your copy of **Eclairs and Lethal Layers** at any good online retailer.

A SANDY BAY 5 COZY MYSTERY

Eclairs
and
Lethal
Layers

AMBER CREWES

ALSO BY AMBER CREWES
THE SANDY BAY COZY MYSTERY SERIES

Apple Pie and Trouble
Brownies and Dark Shadows
Cookies and Buried Secrets
Donuts and Disaster
Éclairs and Lethal Layers
Finger Foods and Missing Legs
Gingerbread and Scary Endings
Hot Chocolate and Cold Bodies
Ice Cream and Guilty Pleasures
Jingle Bells and Deadly Smells
King Cake and Grave Mistakes
Lemon Tarts and Fiery Darts
Muffins and Coffins
Nuts and a Choking Corpse
Orange Mousse and a Fatal Truce
Peaches and Crime
Queen Tarts and a Christmas Nightmare
Rhubarb Pie and Revenge
Slaughter of the Wedding Cake
Tiramisu and Terror
Urchin Dishes and Deadly Wishes
Velvet Cake and Murder
Whoopie Pies and Deadly Lies
Xylose Treats and Killer Sweets

NEWSLETTER SIGNUP

Want **FREE** COPIES OF FUTURE **AMBER CREWES** BOOKS, FIRST NOTIFICATION OF NEW RELEASES, CONTESTS AND GIVEAWAYS?

GO TO THE LINK BELOW TO SIGN UP TO THE NEWSLETTER!

www.AmberCrewes.com/cozylist

Printed in Great Britain
by Amazon